A Substitute Teacher?
No Way!

Lisa McDonald

To order additional copies of this book, contact:
Xlibris
844-714-8691
www.Xlibris.com
Orders@Xlibris.com

ISBN: 978-1-6698-6488-2 (sc)
ISBN: 978-1-6698-6489-9 (hc)
ISBN: 978-1-6698-6487-5 (e)

Library of Congress Control Number: 2023901757

Print information available on the last page

Rev. date: 06/27/2023

I would like to dedicate
this book to Brady.
Thanks for teaching me
I could do anything!

Every morning Emma King

could not wait to see Miss Ring.

Miss Ring took her class on
adventures far and wide.

The class enjoyed the
excitement like a wild ride!

Emma emptied her backpack
and looked around.

But her beloved teacher
could not be found!

All the children stood and read

What the morning message said:

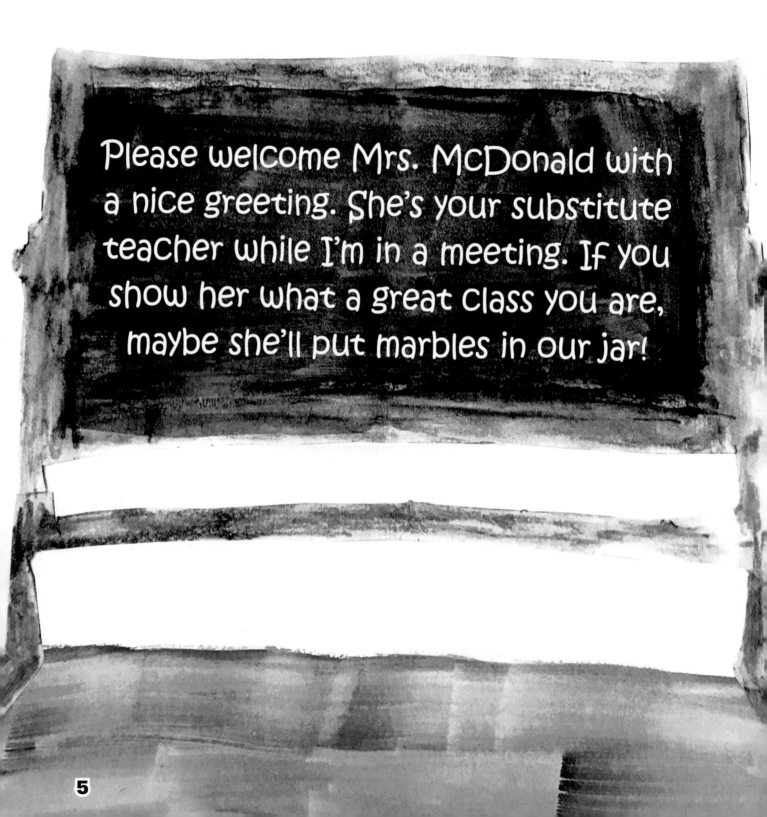

Please welcome Mrs. McDonald with a nice greeting. She's your substitute teacher while I'm in a meeting. If you show her what a great class you are, maybe she'll put marbles in our jar!

Paul cried "A substitute? No Way!

This could be a very bad day!"

Emma felt so full of fright.

She could feel
her face turn white.

She froze and fought

A SCARY thought:

What if I raise my trunk
politely, and she says, "NO"

What if it's an emergency,
and I have to go?

What if I trip, or what if I fall?

She might not make the important call.

**Emma worried her substitute teacher,
would look like a big scary creature.**

What if she has sharp teeth and is green?

What if she is incredibly mean?

"Boys and girls, please sit
quietly on the rug.

I like how it is shaped like a ladybug!"

All Emma could see was
Mrs. McDonalds curls,

So she moved
closer and sat
up front with
the girls.

"Hi, I'm Mrs. McDonald. Let's play a game. Let's think of ways you can remember my name."

John yelled, "Do you own McDonald's? I love their fries!" Mrs. McDonald laughed, "No, but I like their pies."

13

Sofia giggled, "Like Old Macdonald had a Farm?"

"How about young McDonald?"

She answered with charm.

Emma thought Mrs. McDonald wasn't quite so scary. However it was clear Emma was still a bit wary.

"When I teach I pretend
I'm baking a cake.

I follow the plans so
I won't make a mistake."

"You're the ingredients for the special cake.

I make sure I don't over or under bake!"

Emma thought, Wow, I've never
been baked in a cake.

That is a cool adventure I
would like to take!

Mrs. McDonald announced, "If you're good all day, you will earn extra marbles and more time to play!"

Emma shouted, "**Hurray, hurray,** more time to play!

This could be the **bestest ever most funnest day!**"

Throughout the school day, when the class would learn,

not everyone would share or take their turn.

John and Collin kept playing with the blocks after they were told put them in the box!

Brady yelled, as he began to fall,
"Paul made me fall!

He pushed me through the wall!"

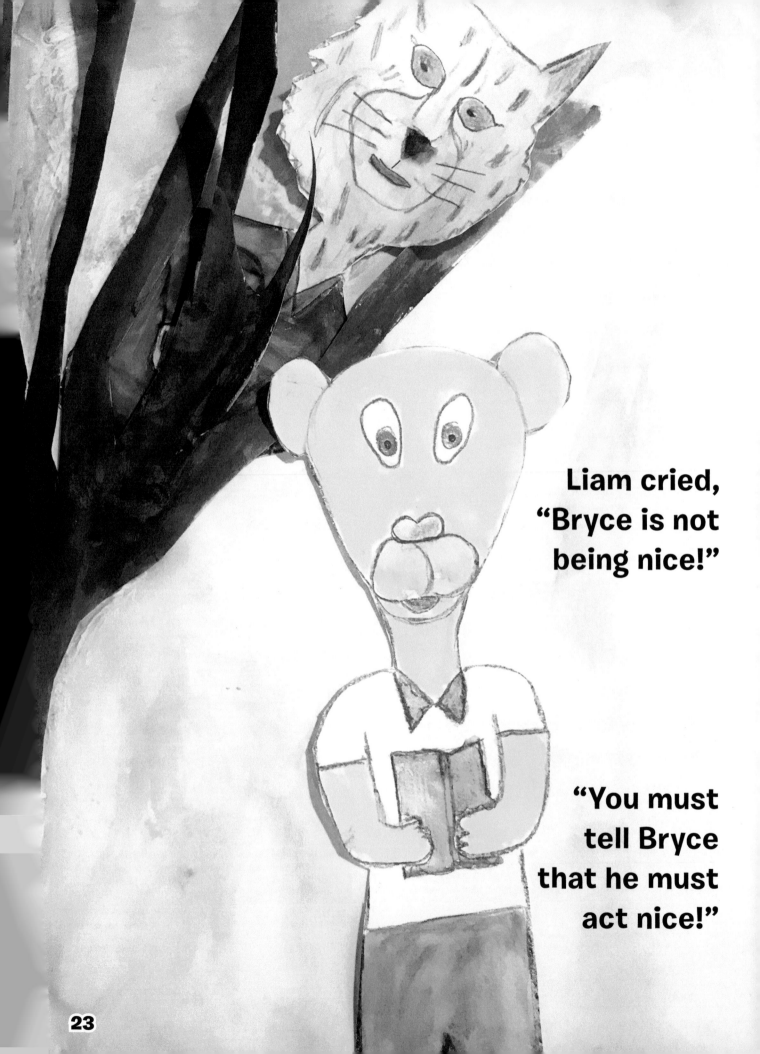

Liam cried,
"Bryce is not
being nice!"

"You must
tell Bryce
that he must
act nice!"

Emma tripped on a ball.

Then she landed on Paul.

Do you think we've earned
extra time to play?

Emma had worried all though the day.

I tried my best to follow the rest!

I didn't mean to trip and fall!

I didn't mean to land on Paul!

Don't worry! For everything that went wrong,

You said, "sorry" and moved on.

"Pack up your backpacks; please show me how!

Quickly and quietly you can get this done now!"

When she saw they were ready,
She was happy to say, "Yes,
you will get extra minutes to play!

You have been fun to teach so far.
Let's add ten marbles to your jar!"

The students had earned
thirty minutes to play.

**They played together
till the end of the day.**

When Miss Ring returned and
blew a whistle, the class knew
it was time for dismissal.

Then Mrs. McDonald waved,
Goodbye!

Some of the class
looked like they
might cry.

Emma said, "You are
terrific and clever!

You really are the best
substitute ever!"

**Emma learned something
this incredible day.**

**Adventures can happen in the
most unexpected way!**

Printed in the United States
by Baker & Taylor Publisher Services